Rob Gil
with his wife an
the Tides of Sha   ....ently working
on various projects including Saturn is for Suckers
Book Two and his Youtube channel.

    Robgilchristbooks.com

    robgilchristbooks@gmail.com

Saturn is for Suckers

This book is dedicated to all those out there that know weird can be good, and as always; Charlie Anne, Meryl, and Salle-Anne who are reminded of that lesson every day.

Special thanks to Adam Wenger and David Arnold

Saturn is for Suckers

Saturn is For Suckers

BOOK ONE

By: Rob Gilchrist

SATURN IS FOR SUCKERS
COPYRIGHT © 2020 BY ROB GILCHRIST
ILLUSTRATION COPYRIGHT © ADAM WENGER 2020

ALL RIGHTS RESERVED. NO PORTION OR PART OF THIS BOOK MAY BE REPRODUCED, COPIED OR TRANSMITTED IN ANY FORM, ELECTRONICALLY OR BY MECHANICAL MEANS, INCLUDING PHOTOCOPYING, RECORDING OR BY ANY INFORMATION STORAGE AND RETRIEVAL SYSTEM WITHOUT THE WRITTEN PERMISSION OF THE AUTHOR.

THIS IS A WORK OF FICTION.

ISBN: 9798618209984

PRINTED IN USA

NOW...ISH?

"Well, I'm from the future, yeah, but don't make a big deal out of it; I mean, we still ride the damn bus."

That made them laugh again. Not surprising. I was saddled up to the middle of a bar full of bearded men in the middle of the afternoon and they were looking for something to laugh at, or fight. I was okay with the laughing for now. It's not like any of them knew they could be liquidated at any moment.

"So, are we talking like Star Wars future, or maybe Alien?" the redneck next to me asked. His breath smelt like paint thinner, and his teeth were a color of brown that didn't belong in the human mouth. Glancing around the bar I noticed we had pulled a small audience. It was everyone in the place. At two in the afternoon there were only seven of us. A bunch of winners.

"Yeah, do you have space ships in the future or teleporters, what's up man?" That question was from the large man behind the bar. I sighed.

"Well, yeah," I said to the man next to me. Turning back to the bartender I attempted not to be condescending. "Don't you have space ships now? It's not too much to imagine that we mastered space travel in the twenties, and it was commercialized by 2030 or so, around when I was born." That incited another gale of laughter.

"So, what about teleporters? Can you just shoot off to whatever planet you want?" Bartender asked again.

"What are you, a child? Teleporter's don't exist. That doesn't make any sense, how would one just shoot across time and space? Magic?" They didn't know how to take that one.

Taking a breath, I surveyed the room. There were numerous animal heads hanging off the walls along with neon signs screaming at the customers to drink their brand of beer. A couple flags hung off the far wall that I vaguely recognized, probably from back when the US had states.

"If you can't teleport across time or space or anything how did you get here? Didn't you say you came from Saturn?" another patron asked. The smile had run away from his face and I had to remind myself that I was unarmed in a bizarre place, maybe try not to nut tap anyone.

"Well I'm almost positive the explosion brought me here, tearing some sort of hole in the fabric of space time, but for all I know, I could have died and we're all in some sort of afterlife-party. Or hell maybe you're all Lariates and you captured me and this is your way of finding out what I know."

They chuckled uneasily. Once again, I considered my predicament. My jeans were blackened with soot, and the t-shirt I wore was speckled with tiny burn holes.

"Can an explosion send someone back in time?" asked the brown toothed redneck.

"And if you were exploded, wouldn't you be dead?" asked another.

"It's a little more complicated than that," I explained. They settled, wanting to hear the tale of the time traveling space man.

"It started in a place like this."

PART ONE: A Place Like This

It smelt of old beer and sweat. The bar was busy, as it usually was on a Friday night. It was around nine, but I had drunk enough beer to have pissed twice in the last twenty minutes. That and the younger girls were starting to avoid the stools closest to me; I had scared off the first few. None of them recognized me and it would take quite a few drinks for them to get curious enough to look me up.

I was still broad-shouldered and tall. My gut was loosening slightly from not exercising as much, but that was alright, we have machines for that kind of thing. Checking the mirror and pulling back my thick black hair, I waved at the bartender.

"Another one Quinn?" asked the friendly bartender. His name was something like Tom, or Tod, or Frank. I'm no good with names. I nodded with a smile and downed the bottle in front of me. Glass bottles were on the way to being banned due to the conservation reforms, but they felt good to hold onto in case a fight broke out. I'm gonna miss those brown fragile shivs.

The place was humming to some new age Asian punk sound that some people considered music, but it wasn't enough to block out the jingle in my ear. Running a finger across my earlobe I answered the call.

"Felix Quinn." I tried to sound sober, but it came off more like a used car salesman.

"Quinn, hey man, its Reggie, what's up bud?"

There were immediately two things wrong with this phone call. First of all, Reggie only calls me when he's loaded and he sounded off, something not quite right. Secondly, and really the more important of the two, he called me bud. That's code for, 'we're fucked'.

"Hey buddy." Time seemed to slow down. I checked out the rest of the place, scanning the long mirror behind the bar. Lots of kids; a few older guys pointing at me and checking their pads to see if they could find a picture before I left; and there in the corner! A clean shaven, dark skinned, middle aged guy in a very new leather jacket. Classic NARC.

"What's happenin?" I asked, trying to make it sound genuine.

"I was talking to the guys down at the club and they wanted to get the gang together for a few beers, you down?" Reggie asked, that shaky voice still as convincing as an inmate who suddenly found Jesus.

Also, the guys at the club absolutely did not want to get together. Well, they may want to hang out with each other, but there is no doubt that they did not want me tagging along. Once you get kicked out of the league for drugs, you're pretty much banned from every angle of the game. Oh yeah; you don't know any of this.

I played ball back in the day. I was okay, not great. When you're okay and not great, playing professional ball, some new performance drug seems like a really good idea. The stuff's called Space Venom. This nasty-looking black tar shit, it's milked from these snakes on Titan. You know, one of the moons of Saturn. Some comic nerd named it Space Venom; I don't know.

When it gets in the human blood stream you can focus, you're stronger, and neurons you killed sixteen parties ago start to fire. It wasn't technically banned when I started using it, but it sure as shit was hard to get. Should have been a warning of some kind, I wasn't paying much attention to anything that wasn't tits or booze, and it caught up with me.

So, with that knowledge fresh in your brain, you can probably understand why the guys at the players club wouldn't exactly be thrilled to have me hanging around. Guys that are sportscasters, and models, and are in buddy comedy movies with soft emotional social messages. Better to distance yourself from the guy who was caught sneaking Venom into the locker room of the semi-finals.

Anyway, the good-looking fellow in the fresh leathers kept glancing my direction. It was time to end this call and ditch him before I got dragged into whatever pile of shit Reggie had stepped in.

"Reg, I'm going to have to call you back." I brushed my earlobe again to end the call. Microtechnology had become all the rage, and I wasn't one to buck the system. Tossing a fifty on the counter, I stood and made my way toward the bathroom, or more importantly, toward the back exit. Leather Jacket stood and followed.

All I had to do at this point was pretend to take a piss, then get to my ride. A baseball bat was sitting shotgun. What? No, not that kind of bat; this was made of advantium. Yes, it does sound made up, mostly because scientists didn't name its properties. When humanity found its way to the farther reaches of space it wasn't scientist who piloted those missions, it was average jerk offs like you and me.

One of said jerk offs stumbled across a metal. He didn't know that it didn't exist on earth; all he knew is that it was light weight and could be used as a weapon. Lucky for us Astro players, it quickly became the material of choice for our bats. Advantium, sounds a lot like advantage, right? Take a wild guess at what douche bag named that metal; athlete or scientist…

Anyway, I had an extremely light weight, extremely durable club in my vehicle that I would have very much liked to get my hands on before Leather Jacket got his hands on me. Instead, I got another call.

"Bitch, did you just hang up on me?" I assumed he didn't really need an answer as I clearly did hang up on his bitch ass.

"The DOJ is looking for you, and now you've got me sequestered in this shit!" As soon as the words were out of his mouth, I heard someone else shouting on the line. They were clearly perturbed that he had outed them.

"Mother fucker, I told you I would call him! I never said he'd be cool with getting together!" Reggie screamed at some invisible tormentor. It confirmed what I had already suspected; someone was trying to get the fix on me. A quick glance over my shoulder confirmed that Leather Jacket was following me toward the bathroom. Either he wanted an old fashioned, or he wanted to see what the inside of my skull looked like. Turning and pointing at the man in the leather jacket I did what anyone would do.

"Is that Jaden Smith?" I shouted, loud enough to cut through any sound system. It took exactly three seconds for people to acknowledge me, then Leather Jacket. He didn't look quite like the actor, but enough that someone with a few drinks in them could make the distinction.

"Holy shit, Jaden!" someone shouted, followed by multiple other call outs. In the blink of an eye there was a wall of half-baked loons between me and my stalker. I bolted. Kicking the back door open I pushed through a crowd of frat boys into the parking lot. My ride wasn't far off.

Slowing down, I put my hand up to my ear and started a fake conversation. A couple in front of me stopped and the blonde dropped her purse.

"Shit woman!" the man shouted, as if dropping her stuff was a tremendous loss to him. The guy turned to me. He looked like a football player, huge.

"Don't run, Felix." His voice was much deeper this time, and they had both turned to me. This time I could see the guns hidden beneath their shirts. I did what anyone would do. I ran.

I woke up an hour or so later. I didn't even have to open my eyes; the smell of piss and vomit let me know immediately that I was in a squad car. When I did open them, I could see the man that I had mistaken for a football player and the woman who played his girlfriend. Shifting slightly, I felt the burn marks on my back from where they had hit me with the taser.

"Mother fuckers, this shirt cost more than you make in a week." I felt like a douchebag for even thinking it, but god damn it, I really liked this one.

"Hey Quinn, just for the record, she's the one who hit you with the fun gun. I was going to take it easy on you, man." Squinting in the mirror, I could tell he wasn't entirely happy about the circumstances. Shifting forward, I settled in and checked myself. Keys and knife were gone. Belt was still on and they left me my boots. That was nice of them.

"He told you not to run," the blonde reminded me.

"Is that what he said? I don't know if you noticed, but I was on the phone." Maybe I could get out of this if the cops had stunned me for no reason whatsoever.

"We heard you. You were just saying applesauce over and over. Not much of a conversation." Blonde called me on that one.

"They do that in the movies, to make it sound like conversation. Maybe I needed a scene partner, or maybe I was really fuckin hungry." The big cop grinned at that one.

"I looked you up when we got the call. Your movie got a 32% on Rotten Tomatoes. Doesn't sound like a scene partner would have helped much." Blonde shot off. This chick was tough.

"Damn Nikki, lay off the man. He's already had his ass kicked tonight." Big cop called for a truce. I was all about it.

The car went quiet after that. My breathing was a little harsh and I realized my face hurt. Rubbing my hand over my nose, I winced. Pushing up on the bridge, I had to fight back tears. Something was wrong up there. When they zapped me, I must have gone down face first. TGIF indeed.

Leaning back, I watched the city pass for a few minutes, trying to block out the burning in my back and throbbing in my nose. I had been drinking in Malibu, but they were driving downtown. The planes and hover cars were getting more frequent in the night sky. We must have been getting close to LAX-COS.

The COS part? Yea that stands for Cosmos. A chunk of the international airports had gotten a little bigger by adding on a Cosmos section. This way it would be much easier to hop on a shuttle to the outer reaches of space. I think the first one was in Japan in the 30s. No, 2030's. Have you been paying attention? This is a story about *your* future. Anyway, they went up fast.

"We getting close? I'm floating back here. Had to split from the bar without hitting the head." They glanced at each other uneasily. That was not comforting.

"Just about there, man." The big guy told me. They gave each other another glance. I'm not sure if it was the look, or the fact that I was about to piss myself, but I sat up. We were definitely at LAX-COS, but we were going in the back way.

"What the fuck?" I asked. Another one of those glances. This wasn't about drugs, or even something incredibly stupid Reg had gotten himself involved with. Someone had shit the bed and I was the toilet paper. Pulling up to a private entrance, Big Cop flashed a badge and the gate opened.

Another car was waiting to lead us to a hanger. A very large hanger. It housed a very expensive vehicle that was essentially a space yacht. The lights in the hanger were turned down low but I could see a small group gathered by the side of the yacht.

Pulling in and circling, Big Cop parked the car and got out. Blonde Cop spent a minute fixing herself up a little, running some color on her lips and fixing her tits.

"You blowing the whole crew or just the pilots?" I asked watching her.

"Have a nice ride, asshole," she said with a thin smile on her face before stepping out of the car and strutting over to the group beside the spacecraft. I'll tell you what, she did have a great caboose.

"Come on Quinn," Big Cop said sadly propping my door open for me. "I saw you play ball; you weren't that bad." I'm not sure if he was trying to make me feel better, but if so, he was bad at it.

Moving toward the waiting group, I could see most of them ogling Blonde Cop, but the ones not looking at her were a little more concerning, they were looking straight at me. Taking a look over my shoulder, I considered another try. The runways stretched out into forever with various colored blinking lights and massive ships dropping in and out, there was no way I was going to make it running this time. Instead I accepted my fate and made my way deeper into the hanger. Two men broke away from the group to meet me and I recognized one of them.

"Felix Quinn!"

The larger one said it like I may have forgotten my name. But I remembered where I knew him from. He was a very tall, very solid, black man with a scar running down the center of his face. At some point he told me it was from a drug raid; I bet he had wrecked his 12 speed.

"Agent Humpback! What are you doing in the banger hanger, come to get your log cutter stretched?" We weren't exactly buddies.

"It's Special Agent Humdack now, and apparently you're still an asshole." He was clearly not impressed by my quick wit.

Humpback, as I so loathingly refer to him, was the DEA agent that got me kicked off the league. Like I said, back in the day, dudes were shooting Venom like it was nothing. A few of us took the big hit and were banned.

Special Agent Humdack had been the man working on a sting operation to find out where the Venom was coming from. Incidentally it led to my team, and then straight to me. I flipped like a little bitch. They were able to stop one of the many providers of the drug into California; and I didn't get raped in prison. Fair enough I suppose.

"Good luck, man," Big Cop whispered giving me a soft pat on the shoulder before turning toward his partner who was still living up the spotlight with the rest of the people in the hanger.

"Officer Goode," Humdack called, stopping him in his tracks. It sounded like goodie, and I had to bite my tongue not to laugh in his face. Goode turned back to the special agent.

"I talked with your Captain; he said I could borrow you for this. I will need an LA officer as a go between. You and your partner were volunteered." He said it all while glancing between Goode and my increasingly swelling nose.

"Sir? I have no authority beyond this port. If you are taking him out, I won't be of any use to you." Goode said it slowly, as if he may be getting off the clock and this was the beginning of a series of shit sandwiches he was about to force down.

"That is correct. However, you and your partner are being given special clearance here to assist with Mr. Quinn. This is a low body count op, and we could use a couple more bodies that know the layout of LA. You will potentially have a part to play here," Humdack explained.

Goode glanced sideways at his partner who was giggling with an older gentleman in army fatigues. It was a look of pure panic. He was more scared of her than anything in the hanger.

"What the hell is this all about? You need me and the coffee and cream dream team over here? Are we taking stock photos for a community college?"

Goode and Humdack glanced at each other. Maybe I should have left the skin color out of it, but hell, nobody was telling me shit.

"Quinn, we have a potential crisis on our hands, and you may very well be able to stop it before it gets worse. Lives are at risk and we need to move fast. Let's get aboard and I will give you and the team a sit-rep." With that, Humdack turned and twirled his finger in the air. The crew scattered, prepping the big rig for take-off.

"Goode-two-shoes, what the fuck have you gotten us into?" I asked the large cop who was trying very hard to become invisible to his partner as Humdack approached her. Blonde Cop was still smiling as Humdack began talking to her, but her smile faded and as her new orders fell into place. The fire in her eyes burned into me.

"I may just hide behind you for a little while," Goode warned me.

Avoiding Blonde Cop's death stares, Goode got me up the ramp and loaded into the yacht. It was set up like a large house: foyer, living areas, kitchen and bedrooms. The middle of the ship had a swimming pool/bar/theater in it. Goode gently pushed me past the lavish stuff as we made our way into the small passenger section of the ship specifically for entering and leaving planetary orbit.

The room sat fifty, but only ten chairs had been pulled out and secured so that they were in a small circle around a round table. Techs were securing everything to the floor for takeoff and I was suddenly getting anxious that I was about to be yanked from this planet without any idea what the next move was. Who was going to feed my fish?

"Quinn, you can have these back, just behave yourself," Humdack told me sliding a plastic bag of my belongings across the table at me.

"Very generous of you," I grumbled, filling my pockets. "You got an IV on board? My nose is killing me."

The IV is one of the gifts from our alien neighbors. It shifts the molecules of our body to heal wounds. Pronounced "IVY", IV is actually the fourth thing we humans found to use the tech for. I'll let you guess what the first three were.

"In the bathroom you passed by the bar," Humdack told me, settling himself in one of the chairs and setting out his Epad. "Officer Goode, please keep an eye on our guest."

Goode nodded, turning back to me with a look of exhausted distain.

"Don't give me that, this wasn't my idea," I told him shuffling back the way we came.

"Out of the way, shit stain," Blonde Cop told me, shoving through the doorway past me. At least everyone was in a cheery mood.

Peeking in a couple doors, I found the bathroom and sequestered myself. Getting a look in the mirror confirmed what I already knew; the nose was broken. A wide gash ran down the left side and my face was stained with blood. Apparently, no one cared too much that I looked like a horror movie extra upon arrival.

The IV looked a bit like a large vibrator and I held it up to my face, letting the familiar hum do its work. My nose itched and I had to stop to sneeze a few times before it was done. Checking myself in the mirror, I smiled. Still got it! Light green eyes, strong jaw, only slightly receding hair, and a nose that wasn't completely destroyed.

Stopping to dig through the drawers I could only find a new toothbrush. That was good enough. Pulling the IV back out, I let it run against the base of the brush long enough for it to look like the brush was vibrating. The molecules were spinning so fast it was hot. Grinding the brush against the sink, I fashioned an old school shiv.

"Come on man. Let's get back, they're waving me over," Goode declared through the bathroom door. Tucking my shiv and putting the IV back in its holster, I moved to the door.

"Oh damn, maybe I should have left it alone. Do you smell like that at the beginning of your shift?" I asked Goode, who gave me a shove toward the passenger section.

"Get settled, we're about to take off," Humdack informed us. There were a few new faces sitting around the table. Most had been hanging out in the hanger, and one was Reggie. Goode sat me down, then set himself between Reg and me.

"Hey *buddy*," I spat out, glaring across the table at my Judas.

"It's not like that, man. These assholes were going to get you."

"We'll debrief once we're in the air," Humdack cut him off. As if on cue, the engines roared to life and panels along the walls faded back, transparent so that everyone inside got a good look as we backed out of the hanger.

Unlike commercial flights, there was no safety briefing, no introduction from the pilots. Our seats simply twisted toward the front of the craft and the seatbelts did their work automatically. A very beefy man in a tight black suit was wrestling with a couple bottles of bourbon, trying to get them into a cup before we took off. His massive hands didn't seem up to the task of removing the tiny lids.

Without any more warning, the craft jumped forward, burning rubber. We were treated to a wonderful view of the dumpsters behind LAX-COS before the secondary engine kicked in and it was hard to watch things anymore. Colors outside melted together and the vibrations rocked hard enough to make some women moan, and young men cream their jeans during takeoff. Someone let out a groan and I watched the big fella grit his teeth as one of the small bottles of bourbon ended up in his lap.

Twenty seconds, that's all it took, then the vibrating stopped. Everything went back to normal and the colors outside were reduced to black. The massive zero gravity billboards that were set up beyond Earth's base atmosphere screamed not to forget your fruit snacks, wherever you may be headed.

"God I hate that." Goode groaned next to me. The large man looked a little green.

"Don't worry, you only have to do it a few more times, like whenever we get to…?" I cut my eyes to Humdack waiting for some answers.

"Pherosis" Humdack answered without looking up.

"Nope! I can't go back there," I demanded immediately forgetting I was buckled in as I failed at standing up.

"Reggie is going back as your contact, but we will need the two of you to get inside and find out where the new strand of Venom is coming from." Humdack said it like talking to toddlers.

"If I go back there, Farrah will know I'm in town within minutes. Then we have a whole new set of problems. Wait, what new strand of Venom?" All eyes twisted back on me. What, was I the only guy who didn't watch the news?

"The strand that is out there, infecting people, and killing them. It's been all over the news." Blonde Cop informed me angrily. God damn it.

As the ship settled into cruising speed, the walls of the vehicle transitioned back to the base interior giving the room a more intimate setting. Lights came on mimicking natural light but the mood definitely changed.

"Well just make some arrests to stop the flow. It can't be that hard, can it?" I asked squirming in my seat like some misplaced sea creature.

"I know you're just here to get us in the door but you can't be stupid enough to think we haven't tried that." It was the big guy with the bourbon. His hands looked like anvils, and he had a face covered with acne scars, but his eyes glared down on me.

"Just get you in the door?" I asked. Maybe that would be doable. Just stay on the surface for a few minutes, get these collars in there and then retreat back to the yacht, or even better, somewhere else far from these people.

"We're going to need cash. They may not be willing to just open up to us after so long away," Reggie added. I cut a look in his direction and he was tapping his fingers against the arm of the chair. Even in the middle of all of this the son of a bitch was trying to rip them off.

"We've got that covered," Humdack told him without even looking in his direction. "Avanti is going to be going in with you. He'll be handling the money part of this operation," Humdack added, motioning to the giant slab of a man with bourbon in his lap.

"You want us to walk into the Play House on Pherosis with a massive bodyguard?" I asked. Cold sweat was breaking out on my back and I gave Avanti a long look. He stared back at me as if his look alone could break my nose again.

"People go into the Play House all the time with body guards and hit men. That's exactly who the place caters to." Humdack was amazing at stating the obvious.

"If anyone tries anything or decides to mess with one of you, I'll break his arms," Avanti added, his voice a deep growl. I wasn't worried about any men on Pherosis, but it didn't seem like the right time to let them know we may be hunted down by a group of vicious biker broads.

"Is Farrah still on Pherosis?" Reggie asked, like he could see into my mind and decided to pull out the worst bits.

"I'm not sure," I stalled, dragging the words out.

"Who's Farrah?" Goode asked, apparently wanting to be injected back into the conversation.

"When we used to come out here, we were royalty man." Reggie started. He didn't get to finish that story.

"Hold on a second spaceman. I just looked it up and this says that there's almost no way aliens could find us without just bumping into us randomly," One of the barbarians at the bar interrupted.

"They can and they did...or will, however you want to look at it." I told him, taking the last of my drink in a large swallow and glancing up at the bartender who was already getting me another.

"This says we're too close to the sun though," he tried again. The sceptic of the bunch, or just an asshole. Everyone else was content with the story so far.

"I can try and explain it to you but it's fairly obvious that you won't know what I'm talking about," I tried again, taking a swig of the fresh drink provided.

"Oh really? Then let's hear it future boy," the hillbilly shot back, his face red from consumption, I could smell the bourbon on him.

"Ok fine, from what I remember from school there are three pieces that need to be used together in order to assume intelligent life. The first is a radio telescope, and that detects radio waves which are primarily used by advanced creatures. Second, you need a spectrometer which essentially gives a planet a chemical fingerprint to help pinpoint. Finally, you need a mechanism that detects sulfuric, carbonic and nitric acids which prove the burning of fossil fuels, something only done by advanced creatures. With these three things combined you can argue that there is a proof of intelligent life. The guys that found us used these three plus another dozen or so readings that let them zero in on our little blue dot."

The room was silent. Everyone turned back to the interrupting redneck and waited for a rebuttal. For a long minute it didn't seem there would be one.

"Well, yeah. I suppose that could work," he said finally under his breath.

"So, Farrah?" the bartender asked. They all seemed to lean in a bit.

"We'll get there. What do you guys know about space pirates?"

"The girls in this place, let me tell you," Reggie went on. That was when the alarm siren started blaring. It gave us about a three second warning before we were hit.

The impact rocked us sideways so hard that Avanti's seatbelt snapped and he was thrown against the wall of the room. He stuck there for a moment as the ship's artificial gravity adjusted to the tilt and swing of the blast.

"Open visors! What did we hit?" Humdack screamed. The walls seemed to melt away and we were left looking at massive chunks of rock and ice. The ship was designed to drift through them with a gas chamber made specifically to push these types of threats away. Regardless of all that bad-ass tech, a rock the size of a school bus was forcing its way through the gas cloud toward us.

"Starboard gas, hit it at maximum!" someone shouted from the cockpit of the ship. The gas cloud thickened and the piece of rock slowed, but it still hit us and we were all rocked sideways again like in some cheap movie.

"There!" Goode shouted over the screaming alarms. Behind a few floating shards a ship was idling. Its engines were shut off and we could only see the reflection off of its chrome.

"Son of a bitch, pirates!" Humdack shouted back, unstrapping himself and motioning for the rest of us to get out of our seats and follow him. He produced a small pistol and ran for the common space.

Doing as I was told, there was a sudden jump in my stomach as we transitioned rooms. The pool in the middle of the room had dumped some water, but what was left in the pool was at an odd angle instead of flat. Stepping through the threshold I was tugged sideways, and everything felt slightly out of whack.

"The gravity system is fucked," someone said as they ran through the opening and into a room marked 'Crew'.

"You can't use that in here; you'll kill us all!" Blonde cop told Humdack, motioning toward the gun in his hand. The sides of it were glowing a soft white and I realized it was a micro rail gun. It fired tiny rings of metal at insane speeds, designed to break apart in their target.

"I'll get close." Ole Humdack sure as shit wasn't lying about that.

The rest happened fast. Another chunk of ice hit us, then we heard the pops as the pressure dropped. Suction opened up in the room we had been sitting in at takeoff and everyone was off their feet being sucked in that direction. A crewman was trying to get out of that room and was jerked backward into the doorframe. We could hear his spine snap, loud even against the sirens and whoosh of air being sucked out into space. He hung there horizontally, back braced against the door frame.

"Aarg!" the guy screamed, blood sliding out of his mouth and across his face at a defiant angle toward the hole in the hull. "They're coming in, frug encun." He was trying, bless the man, but he was losing too much blood. He gave us the important piece of info: they were coming in.

While the redshirt faded away, we were all grabbing at anything near us to keep from being sucked out into space. The force of the suction was dying slowly and Humdack was carefully moving to the dying man. He didn't help him; instead he crouched down beside his body and waited, giving us a wave that could have meant anything from, 'hey guys' to 'hide'. In hindsight it definitely meant 'hide'.

The first pirate through the door was wearing a thick grey one-piece suit and no helmet. Its head was reptilian with small suckers along both sides of its neck. It was clear this one was first due to its ability to survive in open space. That didn't help it though.

Humdack was up and he swept the creature's legs, knocking it onto its back with a wet cry in a language I couldn't identify. Driving his gun into the creature's chest, Humdack fired two rounds then slid off and twisted back away from the doorway. The creature let out a scream that made my eyes water. Wanting to watch the creature, I was unable; watching the large dark agent move like that was mesmerizing. I had no idea he had it in him.

The second man came through the doorway and stopped as soon as he saw his pal sprawled out on his back. His pulled a short blade from his belt but was stopped short as Humdack grabbed his left arm, yanking him down. The shot made a whistling noise as the gun wasn't placed directly into the guy's skin, but his neck exploded with blue blood.

"I see you, dank skank!" someone screamed from deeper in the room. The suction of the breach had completely ceased and I moved backward until I was against the door of the bathroom I had visited earlier. Blonde cop and Goode were scrambling around the pool table. He started to draw his gun but she shook her head. Almost tripping over the loose cue ball, he leaned down and scooped it up.

Another reptilian creature came through the door, this time cutting sideways and getting away from Humdack before shots could be fired at close range. Behind the reptile a human came through wearing a thin bubble mask that made his face appear milky white. Humdack swung at him but the pirate sidestepped and ducked, easily avoiding the blow.

Avanti appeared out of nowhere and tackled the human, tearing at the seams in his suit. The man let out a terrified scream as the suit was separated and it let out a hiss as it depressurized. Leaning back, Avanti jabbed the man in the face with his palm, sending him flying into the pool that was still trying to right itself. Humdack was dancing with the reptile who had produced a thin rod rippling with blue electricity. Avanti made his way behind the pirate, ready to attack.

Liquid flame shot through the doorway, hitting Avanti and the reptile, who both turned and jumped into the pool. Twisting back to the breach point, Humdack raised his gun which was immediately hit with a razor thin line grappling hook and pulled from his hand. The DEA agent was shocked into inaction and simply stood there watching as the attacker stepped through the doorway.

The man was easily seven feet tall and looked almost human. He was wearing dark denim jeans and a leather vest with leather boots, no protective gear against the perils of space. His skin was ghostly pale and he was covered in tattoos. His head was shaved except for a perfect Mohawk running down the center. Grinning he raised a massive rectangular gun like nothing I had ever seen before and twisted one of the knobs on it before pointing it at Humdack and firing. A misty shockwave erupted from the gun picking Humdack up and throwing him against the wall. He was breathing, but wasn't moving other than that.

"Hello dum-dums," the man shouted with laughter. Goode jumped up from his squat position and threw the cue ball at the pirate. Turning and firing again, the gun sent the billiard ball backward and it struck Blonde Cop in the center of the forehead.

"Nikki!" Goode shouted, twisting to check on his partner.

I was stuck, and as usual now that everything was going sideways, I had no idea where Reggie was. The large pirate was checking out his prisoners and after a long look around the room, his eyes landed on me.

"Well I'll be dipped in skunk shit, we got ourselves a baller," he said, holstering his massive gun into a leather clip on his belt.

Since I didn't think the crying crewman to my left was a ball player, that really only left one option. Also, the big dude had holstered his gun, so at the very least he wasn't planning on killing me; at least not with that weapon.

"You know me?" I asked, trying to sound like I wasn't about to piss myself. Standing up, I glanced at Goode who was trying to make himself smaller as he cradled his partner's head in his hands.

"Quinn, right?" The big man laughed. "I remember reading the headlines from when you got banned. I like a man who cheats the system."

"Well, glad to know you can read at least." I said it without thinking and felt the faint taste of vomit in my mouth. The pirate glared at me, taking a few steps forward. Others were coming in behind him, spreading out and looking for anything of value.

"You got balls on you, I'll give you that," he said gruffly. Another human with the milky face mask moved toward the man with a case of some sort of wine or champagne, and the big guy nodded confirmation.

"Where you want this stuff boss?" another one, this one reptilian asked. He was bowlegged dragging a safe with him. A piece of the thin metal wall the safe had been bolted to made a scratching noise against the floor as it was dragged.

"Cargo. Good find, let's get that open. Blitz, where you at?" the large man shouted. There was no response for a moment, then the big one saw his friend that had been shot in the throat.

"Who got the drop on Blitz?" the big guy asked. I closed my eyes and hung my head, there was nothing great that could come from killing a pirate's buddy. Peeking around the room, I saw a crewwoman gesture to the unconscious Humdack. Tears were running down her cheeks but she didn't know him from Adam.

"This little shit got Blitz?" the boss asked again, moving over to stand over Humdack's unconscious body. "Load him up."

Two of the lizard men picked Humdack up and started moving him toward the opening between the two ships. Shifting slightly, I could see that they had placed some sort of seal around the hole and it led directly into their ship.

"No, please, we thought you were someone else. It wasn't personal," Goode tried explaining. He had set his partner down. Her chest was still moving with shallow breath.

"Oh, it's personal now hombre," the big man told him. "Quinn, you're coming with us too." It wasn't a question.

I tried to protest, but my throat was too dry and, I hadn't really eaten anything solid so it wasn't helping me be confrontational.

"Come on man," Goode started, but the big man's hand when to his large gun and sat there. Goode didn't fight for my safety any more after that.

"Easy way or painful way, Quinn."

"Screw it, probably better off with you anyway," I grumbled getting to my feet.

"That's the spirit!" the big guy laughed. One of the men with the milky masks came over and grabbed my arm, pulling me toward the opening between the two ships.

"Hands off the merchandise, Shitbreath!" the big guy shouted, stepping to block our path.

"Oh, sorry MC, didn't realize," the man mumbled. He wasn't making eye contact with the large pale man, MC.

"No, you didn't, did you Shitbreath? That's cause you don't think. I ought to…" His hand went to the gun on his hip again.

"Please MC, I got this," Shitbreath almost whispered.

MC grinned. His teeth were pointed like a shark's, and from this close I could see that his eyes were a deep yellow.

"Keep in line, boy. I don't want to have to take your legs off," MC told him. This time Shitbreath glared up at him, hate seething out of him.

"I got this, boss."

For some reason that made MC smile bigger. Stepping out of our way, MC started talking with the other pirates about their loot. Shitbreath nodded me forward, being sure not to touch me.

The two reptilians that took Humdack aboard came out of the opening in the ship and we stepped out of their way. I glanced back at Goode, who was watching me with open-faced desperation. There was absolutely nothing he could do.

"Come on, baller," Shitbreath told, me leading the way onto the pirate's ship.

Stepping across the threshold was like going to another planet, one that was still living in the 80's. There was chrome on everything, pictures of pinup girls were glued to the walls, and there were even strands of colored lights hanging from various beams in the ceiling.

Humdack was lying on a small cot against the wall in the large cargo bay. Shitbreath was leading me past when I got an idea.

"Hey Shitbreath, why don't we take off, man? Everyone's on the other ship. I've got cash, credits, coin, whatever currency you're looking for. Screw that MC dude." I put on my best salesman face.

"Murder Cock," Shitbreath muttered, turning around.

"Come again?"

"He calls himself Murder Cock, MC for short, and if I do that, he'll hunt me down and kill all of us. Probably slowly; he likes to tear people's arms and legs off and watch them wiggle around. The guy is nuts.

"Wait…Murder Cock? I…so many questions." I was truly without words.

"He'll tell you sometime if you really want to know. He never shuts up about his various exploits," Shitbreath told me as he turned back around and stepped toward the crew quarters. Well that idea didn't work.

With a glance over my shoulder to make sure no one else was coming aboard, I grabbed the shiv from my pocket. Stepping up, I kicked Shitbreath between the legs as hard as I could. He didn't make a sound; I don't think he could. Falling to his knees and rolling over on his back, he stared up at me, mouth open, gasping for air. I showed him the shiv and placed a finger over my lips. He tried nodding understanding but tears were flowing down his cheeks and he was barely able to breath.

"The airlock." Humdack groaned from his place in the floor. I rushed to his side but he pushed me away, pointing over my shoulder.

A large blue button was glowing and sure as shit it said 'airlock' on it. Next to that was a small black box that was projecting the artificial space around the hole in the other ship and the door in this one. I hit airlock first and the cargo door started to close. It was loud as shit, creaking and popping.

"Hey, what the shit!?" MC growled. His voice was faint, but it was obvious that he knew the sound.

"Later cock murderer!" I shouted back as the door sealed. Looking through the small window, I saw MC run up to and stop at the sealed hole in the ship. His gun was out.

Holding my breath, I hit the button to kill the artificial seal on the other ship. MC was sucked out into space immediately. Within about two seconds a few more of his crew were also sucked out, flailing in surprise. I hit the button again, putting the seal back up, and hopefully saving the rest of the crew on that ship.

"Ok Shitbreath, we're going to wait a few minutes for them to suffocate, then ole Humpback and I are going to go back over there and retake that ship. Got it?"

Apparently, he did not. The man had gotten himself back together and was standing over Humdack, pointing a gun at the agent's face.

"You open that airlock or I kill this one, then blow off your legs and do it myself," Shitbreath threatened.

"Do it," Humdack whispered. Apparently he didn't see how much of a badass hero I was being and he had no faith in my abilities. Probably a good call.

I turned back to the airlock, but before I could hit the button there was a noise like a rock hitting a windshield. We all turned to the long window against the wall. There were drawings of various body parts and stickers of goofy cartoons on it, but most importantly dead center was a small piece of metal attached to the outside. That was bad, but the massive man attached to the other end of the grappling hook was way worse.

We could see the other three members of MC's crew floating further out into the darkness of space, but MC had his grappling hook attached to his wrist and was reeling himself in.

"Oh, sweet Jesus." Shitbreath whimpered. MC hit the window with a thud, boots first. Leaning down so that his face was almost against the glass, he screamed.

"You fucked up boys! Shitbreath, say goodbye to your legs!" MC was clearly very angry about this dereliction of duties, but damn if he didn't look happy about the opportunity to take off someone's legs.

"I'm guessing he's not going to suffocate or freeze out there, huh?" I asked. Shitbreath shook his head. Sheer terror on his face.

"Now may be a good time for that mutiny," Humdack suggested.

"What?" What did he say? Shitbreath, open this door!" MC screamed against the glass.

Instead of opening the door, Shitbreath ran for the crew quarters. Out of fear that he would purge the ship, I made chase. We made it past the bunks into a hall full of discarded tools that were never put away, and into the cockpit littered with trash from previous meals.

"Sit down, we have to get the hell out of here," Shitbreath told me, taking the captain's chair. I did as I was told; getting out of there was a phenomenal idea.

"I'm going to start the engine and hit the accelerator. You push that purple lever all the way up. It will spin us something fierce, but it should get MC off of us," Shitbreath instructed.

"Aye aye captain." I told him. I think he smiled a little, but I couldn't tell through the layers of fear and anxiety on his face, plus the weird milky mask.

There were thuds against the hull of the ship and within seconds MC had pulled himself to the front of the ship and was eye to eye with us through the large windshield.

"If you do this Shitbreath, I'll do so much worse than taking your legs," MC threatened. The man tried to ignore his old boss.

"You're not really making a great argument for yourself there." I tried telling MC.

"As for you, I think I'm going to sell you to the sex traffickers on Titan," he snarled at me.

Looking over, Shitbreath gave me a nod.

"You ready?" he asked.

"Oh yeah, I'm not getting my log cutter stretched."

With the confirmation, MC shouted something else and punched the windshield, but we couldn't hear it over the roar of the engines kicking to life. MC hit again and a tiny crack stretched across the glass.

"Now!" Shitbreath screamed. I pushed the lever and we were moving forward and suddenly rotating clockwise, picking up speed on the rotations.

MC was screaming again but we couldn't hear it. Realizing this, he shut his mouth and glared at me. I like to think it was because he knew he was beat, and was in wonder at the man who had done it. More likely is that he was memorizing my face so he could tear it off at a later date.

Before he was thrown off by the rotation, MC kicked himself away, giving us the double bird as we shot past him, leaving him alone in space.

"Sweet baby Jesus…" I exhaled, not realizing I had been holding the breath in. Easing the purple lever back, we slowed the rotation and leveled out.

"Where were you headed?" Shitbreath asked. He pulled off his mask and I realized that he wasn't human either. His skin was almost translucent blue with flakes of silver running down both cheeks like diamond tears.

"That's a damn good question. Shit…I can call you something else if you want."

"Well, my real name is unpronounceable in your tongue, so just call me Snake."

"I'm not calling you Snake." I closed my eyes as I said it. Jesus.

"Well I really don't give a shit! That psycho has been calling me Shitbreath for the last eight months so call me whatever you want." He turned away fiddling with the controls.

"How about Mike? You kind of look like a Mike, if his dad banged a magic dolphin."

To my surprise he smiled.

"A human name…I like it."

"Alright Mike, I'm going to go check on my beaten caretaker and figure out our next move."

Mike nodded as I moved to the back of the ship.

At some point Humdack had vomited across the cargo bay and it stank to high heaven. I considered calling him Shitbreath for a moment, but it would just get too complicated. Instead I knelt down and helped him up to a sitting position. Bruises were already starting to stand out on his face and I had no doubt that multiple ribs were broken, and he probably had a concussion.

"Those were some serious moves back there Humpback," I told him.

"We need to kill the transmitter, the rest of those pirates could be tracking the ship." His voice was scratchy as if he just swallowed sandpaper.

"I'll get on that in a sec, but we need to figure out a plan. Just shooting through open space will get us in trouble again."

He nodded slowly, seeing the reason in it.

"We stick with the plan. Get us to Pherosis, and we can still stop the spread of the poison."

"You're not going to be happy 'til you're dead are you, Captain America?"

The man had a one-track mind. Problem was, he was right. Nothing had changed really, we had gone from a large team of badasses to three broken chumps. Sounded like enough to stop an underground drug ring aimed at killing humans. Sure.

Or I could always wait until we get this broken bit of law enforcement to a hospital and I can slip off into the night. Of course, they'll come back looking for me wouldn't they…choices choices.

"They won't hurt the rest of the ship's crew. More than likely they'll ransom them off and steal anything of value. We need to keep moving before they have a chance to chase us down."

Humdack was right. No point in waiting for the pirates to use the super space yacht against us.

"We're going to have to make a stop somewhere on Pherosis before we meet up with Farrah," I grumbled.

"What do you need?"

"I don't know, some flowers or some shit. We kinda had a fight when I left."

When I say fight, I don't mean fight like between normal humans on Earth. Farrah is part elemental. So, when she decides to, she can pretty much pull fire out of nothing. It's a pretty cool thing to see, until you piss her off and she ends up burning down the apartment building you've been staying in the last few weeks. Including burning up your collection of retro video games. Neither of us wanted to take the blame for that argument, and we hadn't talked since the ash settled.

"Oh, we're going to Pherosis? I have just the thing!" Mike chimed in. He was hanging out in the doorway to the cargo bay, not quite wanting to intrude on our conversation but doing it anyway.

"What you got Mikey?" I asked, happy to turn away from Humdack's grim reality.

"You're gonna love it," he promised.

"Can we take a beat here real quick and address this Murder Cock thing?" a waitress asked. She must have snuck in while I was running through the story, but there were murmurs of agreement.

"Yeah man. You had me into it, then you pull out these guys called Murder Cock and Shitbreath. Kind of went a little out into left field, didn't you?" the bartender asked.

I rubbed my eyes, suddenly exhausted. My hands smelt like burned out circuitry, I'm sure that's not cancer forming or anything.

"Listen guys…and gal; I don't name these people. Ole MC wanted that name, and poor Mike was stuck with his nickname because Murder Cock is completely insane. I got him fixed up with a brand-new human name, lickety-split."

Why does everyone think I'm the one naming these people? Hell, my name is half crazy and pirates weren't even involved in that, as far as I know. They're going to lose their shit when they hear about Farrah's friends.

"Another question: These people that you ran into, MC and Mike? What are they, aliens?" This was the genius at the end of the bar who wanted to talk about how hard it was to find life on another planet.

"They sure as shit weren't from Texas," I told him, nodding to the bartender for another beverage.

"So where were they from? I mean, you've got lizard guys, MC, Mike is blue for shit's sake. That's three different races right there. What's the deal with that?" he followed up.

"You think if you took a kangaroo from Australia and dumped it off in Oregon that it would have the same reaction? How about a house cat and you just dropped it off in the living room of your neighbor's house? These things are relative, man. Once we get connected to the rest of the universe you really stop giving a shit about that kind of stuff. Also, I think it's probably a little rude to ask someone what they are. It's a hell of a thing to throw at someone."

They grumbled again, apparently not happy with my answer.

"What about the elemental thing?" a big, hairy patron asked.

"Yeah, you guys are going to like Farrah."

"This is transport vessel CKLV19 requesting permission to land." Mike was squeezing the small handheld microphone so hard he was shaking.

We had slowed to a hover outside the orbit of a service station clinging to the side of a small moon. Stopping so soon was not ideal, but driving around in MC's vehicle didn't seem all that great either. Humdack was making an executive call.

"CKLV19, I am seeing that your vehicle is on the seize or destroy list. State your business; fighters are being mobilized," a sexy voice told us from air control.

"Shit, I knew it. We're in MC's ship. These guys are going to shoot us out of the air rather than risk MC still being aboard," Mike whined tossing the mic down.

Pushing him aside I took over.

"Control, this ship is not the problem; the man who was running it was. He attacked us and we were able to get the upper hand. This is not our vehicle and we need to touch down and regroup. You can have the ship." I glanced back at Humdack, who gave me a thumbs-up.

Mike plopped down in the captain's chair, defeat washing over him.

"You can have the ship? What the hell?" Mike grumbled. I barely heard him. The silence on the other end of the line was deafening. Maybe we should turn around and haul balls.

"Ship CKLV19, permission granted. The fighters will escort you to the harbor. You are considered a threat until we are able to verify your story. Confirm." The sexy voice was back and it was good news.

"Confirmed, thank you, control." I almost sang it. Having to go to stop so soon sucked, but being blown up would suck a lot worse. Glancing at Mike who was still slouched in his chair, I decided to take over flight duties.

"What kind of weaponry is on board?" Humdack asked Mike.

"Not much; we took most of it over when raiding your ship. I've got a pistol, and I'm sure MC's got something or other in his cabin, but I don't want to go in there," Mike told him timidly, as if even saying the man's name would make him appear.

"Keep your pistol tucked. They'll likely search us, but if this goes well, they'll give it back," Humdack explained, nodding me away.

"You want me to go search the big crazy guy's room?" I would have been annoyed if I wasn't anxiously excited.

"Make it quick; I can see the pad at the harbor."

Glancing through the cracked windshield, I realized he was right. A few figures stood on a large landing pad waiting for us. The unmistakable shapes of guns were held across chests. With a half salute, I made my way back down the hall but turned left and went up a ladder that led to MC's cabin. As soon as I got outside the door, I could smell it. I'm not sure what 'it' was, but…damn. Covering my face with my shirt, I pushed the door open.

"Sweet Whiskey Jesus," I muttered. The place was covered completely with crazy amounts of porn and trade magazines. A lumpy looking mattress lay on the floor in the corner, and a desk sat near the back. Large divots pressed into the top of the desk from whenever MC did whatever it is he did in there. Sticking out of the top of the desk was a massive knife. I started to pull it out before realizing that I probably didn't want my prints on that. Behind that on the floor was a big black helmet. I started to laugh; it had a built-in section just for the psycho's mohawk. The guy would never have helmet hair with that thing…or he always did, either way.

Pushing the desk aside I found what I was looking for; a hidden compartment built into the floor. Cracking it open, I gasped. It looked like a dead body at first, but then it started floating. Who the hell fills a sex doll with helium? The doll stared at me with its open mouth as it bumped into the ceiling and got caught in the lights. Tucked underneath, were various-sized guns, knives, odd toys, and what looked like some sort of slime.

I started to reach for the biggest thing on the menu before realizing it was a net launcher and wouldn't do me much good. Next up was a yo-yo. I stood and dangled it from my finger, hoping for a laser of some kind; nope, just a damn yo-yo. The ship shifted and I knew we would be landing any second so I just grabbed a small handheld pistol that was light green with a funky translucent barrel. Tucking it into my pants, I slammed the door shut and shifted the desk back over the compartment.

"How we looking?" I asked, sliding back into the cockpit. The bubble that encased the loading bay had opened and Mike was easing us down. Two small mechs were standing at attention. They were just steel and glowing red eyes cradling large guns across their metal chests. As the bubble depressurized, a creature came out the bay door. She was tall and dark green with long tentacles drooping down from her face over a large blob-like body.

"Quinn." Humdack was gesturing me over quietly.

"What's up?" I asked expecting some reassurance or perhaps a gentle word of wisdom. He grimaced as he pushed himself back up.

"If things go bad..." He dragged a finger across his throat and pointed at Mike. If shit goes sideways, give up the pirate. I nodded my understanding feeling a weird pang of sympathy for our own member of the Blue Man Group. As usual though, Humpback was right; the guy kidnapped us after all and that was a part of why we were stuck outside this shitty service station. Nodding I moved back to the front and took a breath. We were landing.

"Exit the vehicle with your hands above your head." It was sexy voice from the control room. Damn, the dark green tentacle monster did not fit that voice. She was a radio gal if I've ever seen one.

Saturn is for Suckers

Helping Humdack to his feet, we made our way down the ramp as Mike opened it and strutted off the ship like only a pirate could. Guns scanned us since it was impossible to keep my hands up, and support Humdack's weight, but the tentacle woman with the voice of an angel called off the dogs.

"Humdack? You're injured. Alert medical." As she said it, one of the mech's eyes turned blue and it confirmed that medical was on its way. Cool.

"Do you know everyone?" I panted, letting him take some of his weight off of me as the mech approached and lent a hand. As usual, Humdack ignored me completely.

"Evie, how are you sweetheart?" He tried out a smile that wouldn't convince a two-year-old but Evie didn't seem to mind. She smiled back and I had to suppress a groan. Her mouth was full of round yellow chompers that didn't make any sense.

"What am I looking at here?" Evie asked, stepping up and giving Mike and me a long look over.

"We are here on business. Got rundown by some pirates, their boss was a bad one, goes by M.C. We need to regroup so that we can keep moving. Can you help us out with that?" He didn't get into details. What a pro.

"Murdercock? What an asshole. Of course, let's get you situated. I'm going to impound the ship; do you need anything from it?"

With a groan, Humdack motioned the mech to get moving.

"I think we have everything we need; Quinn here can answer any questions you have. I'll come see you when I'm back on my feet." He looked like he was ready to puke or shit or both. With a nod from Evie, the Mechs made off with our escort, and the large metal door slid shut behind them.

"So, what's your story handsome?" Evie asked, sliding up against Mike. He suddenly developed a speech impediment.

"This is Mike, I'm Quinn, and we're really not allowed to say much. I do have a question though. If you're impounding this ship, how are we supposed...?" Evie cut me off.

"There are expenses built in for your government types. We have transport for you, but there's no need to rush is there?" The green woman creature didn't even look my direction; she was eye fucking Mike so hard I was afraid she'd get pregnant. Mike glanced at me, terror in his eyes, begging for help.

"Well I need to clean up, is there somewhere I could go, maybe even a room?" I asked.

Saturn is for Suckers

"Go tell Brooks at the front desk to give you one of Humdack's rooms." She told me licking her lips. "Can I show you the rest of the station?" she asked Mike.

"I...um, we should probably..." Mike wasn't doing great, so I helped him out.

"You guys take your time. I'm going clean up and see if I can't find some grub. Have fun!" I almost skipped away. I didn't want to give Mike time to form a rebuttal.

"Oh, we will. Why don't you show me the workings of this ship...Mike, is it?" Evie cooed.

He was a pirate, and we didn't kill him, so he needed at least a little slap on the wrist. Mike's face started turning yellow, but like my mom always said, 'fuck 'em'.

Inside the service station was a bustle of activity and energy. It felt like an intergalactic shopping mall. The large desk stretched out demanding cash for entry, but behind that was a massive corridor. Multiple levels of balconies stacked out beyond: stores, eateries, and various entertainment suites, people were on small transport devices and walking, running; the place was wild. Neon was a theme for some reason, and it made my eyes hurt a little.

"Help you?" a large creature covered completely in hair asked. He looked like a body builder fucked Cousin It from the Addams Family.

"You Brooks?" I asked back, searching for its eyes inside the fur covered head.

"That's right."

"I need one of Humdack's rooms," I told himI I literally couldn't tell if he was looking at me or in another direction.

"Government lodge. Seventh floor, this card comes with 600 credits." He slid a small green card across the counter to me along with an envelope with what I assumed was my room number. Brooks turned away and as far as he was concerned, I was dead to the world.

"Thanks, haircut," I offered to no response. Shrugging, I made my way out into the pandemonium.

A group of young men were huddled near the elevators discussing if they should enter a place called The Wetlands. I assume it wasn't an agriculture-based establishment. One of them held a woman named Tonya in high regard. A slurping sound pulled my attention away and I looked up in time to see a creature with long, stretched tentacles pull itself over the lobby by means of sticking to the opposite balcony. Under the right circumstances, this place could be fun.

The elevator dinged and I had to side step as a cacophony of characters exited. There were definitely a lot of sexy looking aliens that I silently assumed worked somewhere on the station. Grabbing at my junk, a tiny pink-skinned hottie giggled as she passed. She looked like she could be a child until she turned around and blew me a kiss. That was a face with some time on it, and it was amazing she wasn't falling down with how top heavy she was. Four foot nothing with double D's. My kinda place.

The elevator took me up past the mall-like balconies and dumped me into a red and white washed hallway. Of course, the room was at the very end of the hall, but at least it dulled the roar of the madness downstairs.

"Welcome back Agent Humdack." I read the card out loud in amused admiration. The little green gal had gotten a cookie bouquet up here before I could even make it up. Popping one of the cookies in my mouth, I scanned the other material that had been left for us. One of the sheets had a code on it from medical. Turning on the TV, I punched in the code and it gave me on update of how Humdack was doing.

'Humdack, Gregory.'

'Condition: Stable'

'Broken ribs, internal bleeding, ruptured kidney'

'IV in use, ETA discharge, 32 minutes'

Gregory? What a little bitch. Though the guy was a trooper if he was running around the way he was with a ruptured kidney. Ole M.C. really gave him the business when he got ahold of him. Although, Humdack was executing his pals as they came through the door. Whatever. Anyway, I had 32 minutes before I had to answer to anything and I was going to use it.

Hopping in the shower, I gave myself a once-over then found some clothes set up in the closet. The basic white shirt and jeans cost me 50 credits, but I still had 550 left over for fun. Scrawling a note to Mike and Humdack that I'd be out and about, I left the room, not realizing how good I had it at that moment.

My first thought was to find that little pink lady that grazed my junk. Obviously, she was down to clown. However, when I stepped off the elevator on the second floor my ideas changed a little bit. Directly across from the elevator stood a game casino. This is a casino that follows most of the rules from your basic arcade or Dave and Busters type establishment except you bet on how well you'll do at any given game.

Strolling in to Pay Out I flicked the plastic card with my credits on it between my fingers, glancing between my options. There were the obvious old school video games where big nostalgic types were typing in their wagers for how fast they could clear a level, or how high their score would be. Then there were the county fair style games, my time to shine. I warmed up on some ski-ball, then I heard it. A crack somewhere over my left shoulder. It was the sound of a bat hitting a ball.

"High score bitches!" a kid probably in his early twenties screamed back at his band of buddies. There were seven of them gathered around the small cage that separated the onlookers from the swinging bat and speeding balls. More were gathering around to see what the commotion was about.

"Alright, that's the Earth high score. Double or nothin' on Saturn?" The question was posed by a fat spider looking thing that was hanging off the side of the cage, a thick unlit cigar hanging out of his mouth.

High Score kid twisted around to the gathering crowd that was getting a little excited about the whole thing. Women were giving out drinks to those gathered and I made sure I grabbed something that wasn't blue. High Score kid pretended to give it some thought but it was obvious he was going for it.

"Saturn's for suckers, baby! Let's do this!" High Score shouted, dragging the wood bat against the side of the cage. His entourage screamed encouragement.

"You got it, champ," Spider carny told him, scuttling across the side of the cage and turning some knobs.

High Score kid raised his arms to scattered cheers then lined up over the home plate. The first ball shot right past him, he barely got his shoulders dipped before he realized it was too late.

"Hey, that's bullshit. I was barely ready!" High Score shouted at the spider man. Shrugging, the spider crossed two of his arms and chewed on his cigar.

Setting up, High Score saw the second ball coming and got a piece of it, but it went foul and no points popped up on the red scoreboard. The cheers died down and High Score made a low guttural noise.

"Ball three!" Spider sung down to him. High Score gave him a venomous look but didn't respond.

The ball went a little wide but High Score got a piece of it. The red score-board that had a blinking 300 on it went spinning and landed on 196.

"Oh no, 196, not quite enough to beat the 300. Better luck next time champ." The spider mocked his loser.

"Hey! I want one more, that first ball was bullshit!" High Score demanded. The spider grinned at the challenge and surveyed the crowd. Seemed like he could probably get more business if he gave the kid another chance, so he nodded.

"You know what, I don't know why, but I'm gonna give you one more. Make it count, kid." Spider told him, turning back to the pitching machine.

High Count lined up and flexed against the bat. As soon as the ball was released the kid swung and I knew were this was going. He connected, perfect hit, but the bat was made of wood and the ball tore right through it. The bat essentially exploded, showering the onlookers with splinters. Onlookers lost it, screaming and cheering, but the sounds dissolved when they saw where the ball ended up. It had dropped and bounced maybe three feet in front of High Score. Glancing up at the score board I saw the numbers slowly tick up to 19.

"You got all of that one kid, but some of these guys bite back." Spider laughed. High Score gave him the finger as he stepped out of the batting cage.

"Anyone else want to try their luck? I'll give you the same deal, 300 credit buy in, get 900 if you beat the high score." High Score's buddies were patting him on the back and urging him to get back in there. Someone brought him a shot of some booze and that was pretty much the end of his run.

"I'll give it a shot." I threw my hand up. The spider carny nodded and his smile grew wider. He saw someone even a decade older than the last loser. Easy money, right?

"Step in, scan your card, and pick your bat." Spider told me. "We're playing for 300 points on Saturn." Nodding, I moved over to the bat rack. Most of them were wood, but tucked in back was a jet-black bat with a sheen I recognized. The advantium wouldn't shatter at Saturn velocities. Turning to the plate, I could see the smile on Spider's face faulter for a split second, but he was a professional.

"Ready when you are, slick," I told the creature.

Just like last time, the first ball shot over the plate before I was even set. That was to be expected, carnival games and all. Pushing my concentration down onto the pitching machine I twisted my ankle and waited.

It came fast and I got a hold of it. The crowd was still there and they were cheering, even High Score shouted encouragement against that crooked spider asshole. The noise rose as the red numbers on the score board shot up, and finally stopped.

"287. Not quite there. You have one more ball, Ace," Spider told me. He wasn't grinning any more, and thick saliva was caked around his cigar. The crowd let out a moan, but it was still hopeful. Taking two steps backward from the pitching machine, I tried to concentrate. It had been a while, but like riding a bike, the sport never really leaves you. When the ball came, I saw it with perfect clarity and my body moved on its own from years of practice. I just had to turn my brain off.

"Hell yea," I muttered as the bat connected. It was a feeling you only get from what would be a home run. I knew it the second I made contact. The crowd lost their minds. Looking up, I heard the cheers get bigger and more aggressive as the scoreboard passed 300 and finally settled on 463."

"Alright, alright. Take your credits and beat it." Spider was waving me on. One of his hairy arms wiggled through the fence, holding out three cards that each held 200 credits on them.

"You sure you don't want a double or nothing on Jupiter?" I asked him. He poked me in the chest with the credits and I took them, a smile on my face.

"Here you go man, when the gravity went up on Saturn you needed to swap out bats." I told High Score, handing him one of the cards with 200 credits on it.

"Thanks man, you crushed that cheating son of a bitch. Here." He handed me one of the random blue drinks I had been avoiding, and it just seemed rude to not down it. Wiping my chin, I bid them good luck and went on my way.

Pausing to watch a guy hip thrust his way to a pinball victory, I gave him the obligatory high five on my way out. There was no way to figure how much time had passed as the top of the building was glass looking out into space and the inside was lit like a kid's room. Popping into a clothing store I found a faux leather jacket that didn't pull too many credits off my card.

"If you were gonna party when you get off work, where would you go?" I asked the long-snouted, fur-covered gentleman behind the counter. It was hard to understand with him talking, and using both of his tongues at once, but I was able to work it out. Jinkie's.

Stopping at an interactive map in a glass pedestal I scanned the various alphabets, selecting Earth/English. It didn't take long; Jinkie's was shown as a large pink building with blinking lights on it that were supposed to resemble nipples, although they weren't the best representation. It was one floor down, so I decided to take the stairs this time.

Opening the stair well I was accosted by a smell that could only be described as livestock. There were various trails and footprints along the steps that looked moist, and there was some sort of dripping sound higher up. Instead of sticking around to enjoy the sights, I hoofed it down two at a time. In the stair landing two guys were making out, but I'm fairly certain that at least one of them was a shape shifter as he had size D tits, a massive beard, and a tail.

Shouldering the door open, I was greeted with somewhat fresher air and then immediately smacked into a small pink creature who balked at my sudden arrival.

"Hey, I was looking for you!" I exclaimed, surprised to bump into the same pink chick so quickly.

"Dan tak, fara chumpa!" She shouted at me, waving me out of her way and moving on. Maybe that wasn't the same pink chick. Does that make me racist? Is there a word for that?

Shaking my head clear of the stairs and the run in, I continued forward past a number of tech stores sporting items I may actually be interested in later, when the blood would return north of my neck. Hanging a right, I stopped. There it was, a large pale pink façade with glowing balls hanging off the front. I hoped those were supposed to be nipples.

There were bar height tables off to the side where a coffee shop was slinging caffeine, but I kept my eyes on the prize. A massive grey-skinned creature that resembled the bottom of my foot stood barring the entrance. He kind of looked like a rhino fucked an old lady, or vice versa if she was spry.

"250 credits, mate," he demanded, holding out a three-fingered hand. Swiping my card and handing me a wad of bills, he ushered me inside.

Squeezing past a few more of the rhino creatures, I noticed they were watching their smart watches. People playing games, getting dances, and much darker stuff was apparently going on behind these walls. One of them puffed out his nostrils when he realized I was watching and I got the message, move it along.

Turning a corner, it went from security central to sextopia. Creatures of every different make and model were prancing and shaking whatever appendages they had to shake and to be honest, it was a beautiful sight. A female with birdlike features, wings and covered in feathers approached me.

"What can I get you, hun?" She smiled, at least I think so, with her hardened beak mouth.

"Your English is impeccable," I told her smiling back, "A bourbon, double, easy ice." I said, handing her my card with credits on it. Probably wouldn't get that back, but it's ok, it was on Humpback's dime.

"Interest you in a dance?" a voice asked from behind me. Turning, I had to muffle a surprised cry. It was probably a she, but she was a deep purple blob, bobbing up and down on tentacles. Her face and most of her blob body looked moist, and she was smoking some sort of electronic cigarette.

"You know what, I just got in, I'm looking for my friend; maybe in a little bit," I told her barreling backward in full retreat mode. Without a word she turned and moved to the next mark. This obviously wasn't her first night on the job.

Picking out a small table on the outer ring of the large room I observed the center stage, coupled by two smaller stages. There were dancers on all three grinding to some song that sounded vaguely familiar but I couldn't place. Men, women, and creatures of all forms were living it up, down in the center area. Above them others were getting table dances and bottle service at a balcony bar. I smiled for a moment, forgetting why I was there in the first place. Then I turned to the small television on the wall.

It was set so that you could see behind the bar through a CCTV. Sexy bartenders were making drinks and fanning themselves as they worked, but in a picture-in-picture box at the bottom of the screen, news was running. The headline that caught my eye was '37 dead in drug bust gone wrong' Behind the reporter there was a burning warehouse and bodies could be seen covered in black goo. Space Venom. So, it was as bad as they said. Shit.

"Your drink hun," I downed it and nodded to her for another. This wasn't anything new to her as she simply took the glass and turned back toward the bar.

"Don't I know you?" a very attractive woman asked, sliding into the booth across from me. She was wearing a translucent frilly number and looked all of about twenty-one. I could tell she was a space station baby as she had the tattoos along her neck and a port just to the side of her jugular. The ports are essentially life support in case shit goes sideways. Plug that thing into one of the emergency station supply wires and you can stay alive in open space for a few weeks.

"Is that your sales tactic, lure them in with familiarity, then get them in the back room?" I asked, trying not to stare straight into her nipples.

"Actually no, if you've met me honey, you'd never forget. No one forgets Traea. You though, I know you from somewhere. What do you do?" she asked, squinting at me.

"Consulting work." I didn't exactly lie.

"No, I've seen you on TV haven't I?"

She was getting warmer. My eyes were adjusting to the dark and I could see small white scars on the backside of her neck. At some point she had been exposed to the harshness of space and revived. Tough broad.

"You know, I did do one of those commercials for natural male enhancement back in the day. Maybe that's it," I told her plastering on one of my horniest smiles. She smiled back uncertainly. Then she got it.

"You're a sports guy, aren't you?" Her eyes moved to my neck and shoulders. I wasn't in the same shape as when I played ball, but I hadn't completely let myself go either.

"I may have played a little ball back in the day, but nothing too exciting," I lied. Her smile came back full force.

"We don't get many celebrities in here. How about a dance, half off?" Seeing the hesitation in my face, she was not ready to give up. Standing so that I could see her lean body, she slid into my side of the booth rubbing up against me.

"Well, I'm kind of waiting for someone," I told her. There was no conviction in my voice and she could smell it, like blood to a shark.

"It would be a lot more fun to wait for your friend in the back with me, wouldn't it?" Sneaking her hand on my thigh she started rubbing gently. Shit.

"Well hell."

She shrieked gleefully, grabbing my hand and tugging me out of the booth. Reaching back, I was able to grab my drink before the surprisingly strong little thing got me half way across the room. Another of the large grey creatures barred the way to a much darker back room. Traea whispered something to the big guy and he nodded, clicking on his smart watch before stepping aside. I could feel the credits on my card being plucked away as we made our way into the dark.

A hallway separated multiple large rooms that had couches along every wall. Various dances were happening and I almost stopped completely to see how some of them played out. Something that looked like a large face hugger from the Alien movies was upside down on another creature's crotch and they were getting after it. That's a show I'd pay to see.

"In here, hun," Traea cooed in my ear. The room was just as large and dark as the others but there were dividers keeping the customers separate from each other. I let her push me down onto a couch and tried not to think about what levels of goo I may be sitting in. Tipping my glass up so that I would finish, she took it and produced another bottle of brown liquor from over my head and gave me a refill, at a healthy mark-up I'm sure. I took a sip and decided it was worth it. It was much better than what they were handing out up front.

"If she says hand up, you put your hands up. Other than that, do as the lady asks and enjoy yourself," a thickly-accented man told me, peeking his head into the room. I nodded and he disappeared. Nothing like a random stranger telling you to behave to get the sexy juices flowing.

"Don't mind Rick, you can do whatever you want." Traea winked at me in the dim light and suddenly the music was turned up and the entire room seemed to be vibrating.

Taking another drink, I leaned back and tried to relax. At the very least I was getting free drinks and lap danced on Humdack's line of credit. That was a win no matter how you look at it. Draining the glass, Traea took it from me and set it aside. Then she took my hands and smacked them high up on her hips. She leaned in, rubbing her nipples against my lips and I was finally able to start enjoying myself.

"Do you like that?" She whispered in my ear, flicking the lobe with her tongue. I grunted in agreement and her hand slid between my legs.

"You definitely like that." I could see the whites of her teeth as she smiled in the dark. She wasn't wrong.

"Maybe there's something else that I can get you while you're staying here," she suggested leaning back and thrusting her pelvis into mine. I shook my head. That there was a slippery slope. Had she dug into my past while I wasn't paying attention?

"I'm good sweet heart, maybe we just." But I wasn't able to finish that sentence. Instead we were tossed upward, cracking our heads into each other. I bit the shit out of my tongue and her nose exploded blood.

"Oh fuck, what the hell?" She slapped at me as if I was some sort of bucking bull instead of another victim.

"What the hell was that?" I asked. It was more slurred and I could taste the sour blood in my mouth. Then we were rocked sideways, and her eyes lit up with acknowledgment. I was able to get an arm around her side and keep her from tumbling to the floor, but we were clearly done with sexy time.

"We got hit with something," She said nasally clamping her hand back over her bloody nose.

"Does this happen often?" I asked imagining asteroids, or floating debris slamming into the side of the station. Traea was shaking her head. A large tear had formed in one of her eyes but she wasn't letting it fall. An alarm started blaring overhead and red emergency lights started flashing.

Standing, the lights came on exposing various stages of perversion in the back room. Rubbing the back of my hand across my lips it came back bloody. Traea was still cradling her nose and started making her way back toward the main room. Treating the place like a locker room, I kept my eyes low as I followed her but just like the locker room, you're not going to get out of there without seeing a couple old guys balls.

"Code Orange. Lockdown. Code Orange. Lockdown," a speaker started blaring overhead.

Saturn is for Suckers

"What's that mean?" Traea asked, her voice thickened and nasally. Shrugging, I slipped past her and grabbed the emergency evacuation poster off the wall.

"Black, Blue, Alpha, Red, Echo, Orange...shit." I stopped running down the list of emergency codes and thought back to how it was I ended up in this dive bar of a rest stop.

"Terrorist attack? We're being attacked?" Traea was looking over my shoulder and her voice went up a few octaves as she caught up to the conclusion that I had just come to. As if to make a point, another explosion went off somewhere on the far side of the building. We weren't rocked too hard from that one which meant it was probably internal. Time to hit the road.

"Lockdown, get to the safe room," Rick, the strip tease consigliere demanded, rushing past us.

"Come on, you can be my plus one," Traea told me, urging me toward the back of the establishment. I was a little taken back. Was she being sweet, or did she know there were still credits on my card?

"Well, I hate to say it, but I've got to check on a Humpback," I told her, forcing on a weak smile. She frowned.

"It said terrorists. We have a safe room. Let's just wait it out. We can be safe here." There was no sales spin on this one; she legitimately wanted to keep us safe, and she was scared as hell. Hard to blame her, my fudger was tight as a drum. Glancing at the white scars on her neck, I remembered this gal had been through some shit. PTSD is no joke.

"Go, I'll be back. I have to get my friend," I told her, putting my hand on her shoulder and gently pushing her in the direction Rick had gone. The tears she had been holding back started to drop slowly.

"Let's go T. Safe room. Now," One of the large bouncers from out front demanded stomping down the hall. We could hear cries of surprise and fear from the front of the club now and the entire building shuddered.

"Stay away from the outer walls," Traea warned, giving my hand a squeeze. Turning and following the massive bouncer, her hand went back up to her exposure scars. She glanced over her shoulder and gave me a grim smile before disappearing around the corner.

"Alright dipshit. Let's find ourselves a government agent and get the hell out of here," I told myself. Other dancers and high-end clients were funneling past, giving me funny looks as I talked to myself, but they didn't slow down. This wasn't a place where people stuck their necks out.

Making my way back to the main floor, I wasn't surprised to see that the placed had pretty much cleared out. A few clusters of folks were hunkered down behind the bar or back in some of the booths. The two large grey bouncers from the front door were heading my direction.

"Hey fellas, you got anything on you that could help me get back to my room?" I asked. They exchanged a look that seemed to insinuate that I was joking. Then the one who let me in pulled a small black cylinder out of his pocket and tossed it to me as he continued on his way to the saferoom.

Holding the item up, I saw a small blue button on the side and I held it away from my face pressing it. Nothing happened. Turning it over I realized that it was a steel folding baton. Flicking my wrist, the steel extended a couple feet, locking into place. Pressing the button caused a crackle of electricity to spark at the end, kind of like a cattle prod.

"Awesome, this will come in real handy against a fucking gun," I grunted, always the optimist.

The security hallway was completely empty, and there was an odd silence as I made my way through to the front doors. The floor rumbled beneath my feet and again I glanced at the damn baton in my hand. Someone back in the bar started crying and was hushed immediately. Taking a deep breath, I pushed the door open just enough to slip through and slid out onto my stomach behind the bouncers' area.

The open mall area was chaos. People were running in every direction, hiding, fighting, looting. On top of that there were small pops like gunshots and a low roar underneath it all that I didn't understand. Staying low, I watched as two young men started fighting over a handful of credit cards. They only stopped when a fat slug-like creature slid past, covering them both in a thick yellow goo. Their fury was immediately focused on the bug and they chased it around a corner, disappearing.

"Hey man, tell them to let me in." I just about shocked my own balls trying to turn around at the sudden voice. One of the multiple-tentacled creatures was pulling on the door handles that had apparently locked behind me.

"Sorry man, not my place. I'm trying to make it upstairs," I tried explaining.

"Upstairs? Dude, you got a suite? I'll give you whatever you want if you take me with you. It's a nightmare out there," Tentacle Man explained.

"What the hell happened?" I asked. Sweat was beading up on my forehead.

"That crazy ass terrorist showed up and just started blasting shit. Drove a damn ship straight into the building. Sucked a whole restaurant worth of people out into the dark."

He was talking crazy fast. Adrenaline is a hell of a thing.

"Crazy ass terrorist...you don't mean."

"Murdercock, man! You know, the psycho that has been riding around playing pirate."

"Awesome," I groaned. This trip just kept getting better.

Something roared back toward the entrance of the shopping area and I jumped. A cool wet tentacle brushed against me and I had to fight the urge to throw up. My new tentacled best friend didn't seem to understand personal space. Pushing him away, I stood up and started for the elevator. That was a mistake.

"I like you, little buddy! We should hang out after this if you don't die a brutal death!" A familiar voice screamed. It was followed up by a dumpster, fully engulfed in flame, flying down the main corridor and slamming into the bathroom doors just beyond the strip joint.

"Shit! That's him, we gotta get out of here man!" The creature next to me beckoned.

Glancing up, I could see the balcony above was empty. Remembering the slippery dude that slung himself across the balconies earlier gave me an idea.

"Hey slim, you think you can get ahold of that cross beam up there and pull us up?"

Slim took one look and started moving, speaking softly in an alien tongue I didn't understand. I'm one hundred percent sure it was profanity.

Trying not to slip in his goo trail, I watched as another group of men that had been looting made a run for the elevator across the main hall from us. The first almost made it but was hit in the back of the head with what looked like a computer monitor. Someone threw out a bellow of laughter.

"We need to hurry the hell up..." I started to explain. But when I turned back, Slim was gone. I looked up just in time to see him slime his way over the side of the balcony.

"You shit bag!" I screamed after him.

"Sorry man, every man for himself," he almost whispered back, clearing the support beam and disappearing into a store on the second floor.

"You're not a man! You're a turd with a heartbeat. When I get up there, I'm going to flush your ass down the fuckin john!" I screamed after him. There was another crash from behind me and I turned just in time to see MC jump down from one of the higher balconies and smiled at me.

"Allstar!" he shouted happily, like a kid finding a lost toy.

I cut my eyes to my left; the elevator was only fifteen feet from where I was standing. That was when flames shot out of MC's gun and the doors to the lift began melting like being coated in lava. The insane pirate was blowing on the end of his gun and laughing.

"Oh man, I'm sorry bro. Were you going up?" His pale skin looked even paler; maybe hanging out in the vacuum of space for a while hadn't done him that much good.

"No, you're good. I was actually just hitting the ATM. The surcharge in that place, you wouldn't believe it." I hooked my finger toward the strip club and genuinely smiled. This would be fun if I wasn't about to dump hot pudding in my pants. My other hand was slowly reaching for the green translucent pistol I had taken from MC's cabin. He was too busy laughing and lighting other things on fire to notice.

"All right, put the gun down!" I shouted. In one fluid motion I pulled the green gun and pointed it at MC. My hand was steady but the gun kept going. It was slick like wet glass and flew five feet in the air before coming down in front of me and shattering. I grimaced. That sucks.

"I've got to say, for being a massive pain in my ass, you make this job enjoyable," MC cooed. I couldn't tell if he was telling the truth or not. There was a lot of crazy going on, and his usual mohawk was slightly out of whack. When he turned his head, I could see a gash on the side of his skull. I gave him a grin that I usually reserve for the ladies.

"Was that from me?" I asked, patting myself on the head in the same place as the blood patch. His eyes arched upward and he laughed again.

"No, that was from this crazy ass hairy." He didn't get to finish the statement.

Brooks, the massive hairy creature from the front of the station, flung himself at him.

They both went rolling across the slick floor knocking over boxes outside stores and slamming into the side of the elevators on the other side. Brooks wasn't looking great. Large chunks of hair were burnt off revealing a couple meaty clackers dangling between his legs. They both shouted angrily and MC brought the gun up, popping off one quick burst of flame before Brooks slapped it out of his hands.

MC headbutted the creature and their heads collided with a sound like watermelons slapping each other. Brooks slapped at the fire on his face and I could smell the burning hair. Leaning back, MC drove both legs into Brooks' gut, sending him spinning onto his back.

"I thought you were a big burly bastard, but you're just a cuddly little feller, aren't you?" MC shouted back at Brooks, pushing himself up with clenched fists.

"Cuddly as ever," Brooks grunted, brushing the burned hair out of his face. Underneath the hair his face was wide, almost cave-man-like. Wide forehead, thick jaw, and low sunken eyes. There was no doubt however that he was doing his damnedest to keep things from getting worse.

While they talked and sized each other up, I tried to make myself very small and inch-as quickly as one could, while inching-my way toward MC's gun. It was either that, or I get back upstairs and grab one of those unobtanium bats. I could knock him into next week with one of those bad boys. Brooks seemed to get an idea of what I was doing so he made sure to keep the big man's attention.

"Looks like I got you there," Brooks said pointing at the gash in MC's head. The hairy man didn't seem to express any emotion, but as he pointed with one gnarled claw finger, he smiled.

"Ah damn, look. It's Murdercock!" someone shouted from a balcony at least three stories up. We all looked up where phones and cameras were flashing wildly. The people were scared, but not too scared. Like being at the zoo while the tigers were being fed. Every single one of them thinking, 'there's no way any of that raw natural fury could come back onto little ole me'.

"Get my good side!" MC shouted at them, twisting and flexing his massive right arm. Meanwhile his left arm reached down and patted an empty holster. His eyes darted across the floor before finding me, only a few feet away from his massive cannon.

"Eat shit, freak!" someone shouted, and before MC could take his anger out on me, someone hit him in the side of the head with a mostly-uneaten chili dog. It connected hard against the side of his face, splattering warm chili across his chest and down onto the floor. The dog, with only one bite taken out of it, bounced playfully off his face and made a slapping sound when it came down against the floor. Taking a breath and glaring at me, MC dusted the uneaten bun and cardboard boat tray the dog had come in off his shoulder.

Sidestepping, MC grabbed one of the bar-height tables from the coffee shop and with lightning speed, lunged it upward. Screams echoed throughout the building and we all saw the table clang into the side of the balcony people had just been hanging over, but it didn't look like he did much more than scare the onlookers off. That's when the human arm fell, slamming onto the floor like a dead fish, followed by the splatter of fresh blood. MC turned back to me, grinning.

"Honestly, that was a Hail Mary. I didn't think it was going to go that well. Damn I'm awesome!" he shouted triumphantly, spinning in a quick circle like he was in a dance off no one knew about. He started clapping and gave himself a little bow before the dismembered arm came out of nowhere and slapped him across the face.

"What? Shit! Stop!" Murdercock shouted with confusion, trying to protect his eyes from the slaps. Brooks had picked up the arm and was beating him with it. It was oddly effective as blood was splattering with every swing, coating MC and forcing a retreat.

"Just being a big cuddly bear," Brooks shouted at him. Tossing the arm aside Brooks hit him in the face, hard. MC barreled back and shook his head with surprise. He opened his mouth to speak but Brooks didn't give him the satisfaction. The beast was on him, pummeling, slamming his head, his jaw, neck, and chest.

"Get out of here you creepy hairy son of a bitch!" MC screamed, kicking himself backwards.

Kneeling down, I grabbed the massive gun-it weighed at least fifty pounds-and started studying the dials. That was about the time Brooks tried to put his hands around MC's throat and squeeze.

MC jerked backward hard and kicked Brooks in the nuts. Everyone in the place heard the 'whoof' that he let out, and his hands slipped in the blood on MC's face. With one hard hit to the face, MC sent Brooks sprawling out on the floor. He kicked the cuddly bear in the side of the head hard, but Brooks wasn't done. His eyes were closed, tears streaming from the pain in his swollen nether region, but he got his hands onto MC's leg and swung him sideways like a baseball bat, sending him crashing through the glass storefront of the coffee shop. Screams rang out as hidden baristas thought the end was coming.

Stepping through the new opening, the hairy beast shoved tables and chairs out of the way to get to the bleeding man on the floor. Brooks hit MC in the face as he tried getting up and MC growled. Kicking Brook's legs out from under him, MC grabbed the hairy beast by the back of the head, MC slammed him into the ground. I heard glass crunch and felt the drink in my stomach try to make a reappearance.

"Hey!" MC shouted suddenly, cutting the sounds of battle, still holding Brooks' head against the floor.

I glanced up and realized he was talking to me.

"Yeah, I see you. Don't think you're going anywhere with my gun, Allstar." He said it this time without a smile and a chill ran down my spine.

Brooks didn't make a sound. Instead, he reached up with that clawed hand and dug his fingers into MC's face. Blood ran down into the brown hair that he had left, and MC slapped frantically backward.

"You can't mess with the money maker, Poo Bear," MC told him wiping the blood away from his eye in one furious swipe. Stepping up, MC drove his foot into Brooks's side, sending him sliding across the glass, clicking and grinding. Spitting at the blood running down his face and into his mouth, MC glanced at me just to make sure I hadn't moved, then grabbed the door handle to the coffee shop.

It was a large steel pipe welded into a flat connection that had been bolted to the thick glass. Giving it a yank, MC made a yipping noise of joy when it broke away with a thick piece of glass connected to it, making it look like an insane pizza slice. Glass crunched and MC turned back just in time to side step Brooks, who was lunging for him. This time, Murdercock twisted and brought the piece of glass up, gripping the handle with both hands.

Blood sprayed in a geyser, and Brooks' arms kept swinging. They didn't seem to realize that they, along with the rest of his upper body, were no longer connected to his bottom half. The top half of his body slapped onto the ground like a wet mop and slid another six feet before stopping, giving everything a good coating of fresh gore.

"You made me do that, Teddy," MC told him almost regretfully.

Fresh screams echoed from above them as the onlookers realized what had happened. Glancing at the piece of glass he was holding, MC seemed to consider keeping it for a minute before dropping it to the floor, letting it shatter.

I moved backward slowly. The massive fighter looked dazed; this was the one chance I was going to get. There were absolutely no markings on the gun to let me know what did what so I just left all the settings alone. The stairs I had come down were about twenty feet behind me, and I was already doing a slow-motion version of the moonwalk. The place was completely silent now except for the various music playing in the stores that had survived and the gentle humming of maintenance equipment. I took care with every step not to hit a piece of glass, or anything else that had gone rogue during the battle of the beasts.

"Shoot his ass man, what are you waiting for?" someone shouted from upstairs. It sure as hell wasn't the guy who had thrown the chili dog. That seemed to wake MC up. His shoulders were slouched and his head hung low. He slowly turned to me.

"Thanks fuck face!" I shouted to the guy upstairs.

My first thought was that I could get the gun up and blast this psychotic space pirate before he could even move. The guy was tired from a big fight and didn't look like he had much left in him. My second thought, directly behind that one, was, run.

"All right Baller," MC said groggily. Then he stood up straight, arched his back so that it popped loud enough to make me cringe, and turned toward me.

"Strip club?" I asked him. If my voice would have had a smell it would have been cat piss. Hands sweaty, I thought I was going to lose the gun, so I adjusted it in my grip.

"Don't," MC said, but that was all he got out. The gun made a WHOOM noise and MC was tossed backwards like a piece of cardboard. He flew through the window of a shop that seemed to be exclusively selling socks. His legs caught on a low shelf that must have been bolted to the ground because it flipped him and sent him spiraling backward into the rear of the store with a crash.

"Hell yea!" the fuck face from upstairs screamed, and with him, a roar of approval rained down on me. It was deafening in the enclosed area, and my ears were ringing.

"Shit, shit, shit, shitshitshitshitshit." I was on repeat. Yea, I had accidentally just knocked the shit out of the most brutal man I have ever seen, but...I knew he had a pretty high tolerance for pain. I mean, I left the guy out in space last time. Dropping the gun, I started for the stairs, then changed my mind. It only took a moment to turn around and grab the thing but it felt like forever. Slinging the massive firearm across my forearm, I shuffled to the stairs.

"ALL-STAR BALL-ER!" He half shouted, half sang it in the 'Let's Go, De-Fence' melody. I froze. Only for a moment, because I could see a dark shape rising in the back of the Sock It To Me store. Then I ran.

I got up the first set of stairs and ducked into the first store available. It was a miscellaneous tech store with a bunch of cool looking shit that no one needed. Dropping to a knee, I cranked the dial on the side of the gun clockwise. It made a humming noise then went quiet.

"Please don't kill me," a choked voice from the back of the store whimpered. Jumping to my feet and raising the gun, I slipped into the door, almost falling down. A long trail of slime trailed into the store and I realized it was the coward who had left me earlier.

"I should, but I'm not the one you need to worry about," I told him, moving back out into the hall to take a look. MC was almost to the stairs.

"He's making a move, down the hall!" The creature behind me shouted.

"You shit snake," I hissed, considering using the gun on him. Screw it, I had no idea what the gun was going to do anyway. Stepping into the hall, I could see MC on the stairs. We both froze. There wasn't a smile on his face this time and he was bleeding from multiple places. He held out a hand, palm up.

"Hell with it," I grunted, pulling the trigger. Liquid flame exploded from the barrel of the gun, drenching the stairs and covering the side of the railing. MC jumped back, but there was a hint of a smile on his face. Twisting, I ran. There were more elevators on the far side and that was my destination.

There was a plume of smoke between me and my attacker now.

"He's in the tech store!" I shouted over my shoulder. Suck on that, turd burger.

There was a large thump and glass shattered behind me as MC slammed into the tech store. I could hear the slime creature let out a shriek and then MC was laughing. Smoke was filling the balcony and rolling along the ceiling, which was the next balcony's floor. Somewhere up ahead I heard people shouting, but it didn't matter. I didn't want to know what happened if this brute got a hold of me. I shot more liquid flame along the floor, making the path look like lava. I was running again.

"I guess we'll do it the hard way then." I heard Murdercock shout at me.

Turning, I saw him toss the screaming slime guy over the balcony. Then MC started running. Straight into the flames. Between the fire and smoke, he looked like a demon, and he was grinning like one.

Pulling the gun up, I turned the dial again and leveled the weapon.

"Don't you die?" I asked, pulling the trigger. The gun clicked and with a massive plume of flame, a long steel harpoon was flying out of it. MC avoided it easily, but I barely saw. The blast picked me up and threw me backwards. I had the sensation of flight for just a moment before everything went black.

"Wake up Allstar." I knew the voice at once. Shit.

Opening my eyes, I scanned the room, the familiar faces. We were in MC's rig again, this time with everyone that had been stuck on the old yacht ship. Reggie was against the wall in cuffs, and his mouth was gagged. Goode was cradling his partner who seemed like she'd had better days. A few of his crew remained, at least the ones that hadn't died outright in the last fight. It took a minute to assess all of this because I was completely wrapped in chains and hanging upside down.

"There's my little Allstar. Welcome back wittle bitty baby boy." MC was cooing as I blinked back into consciousness. Well at least he hadn't killed me.

"You brought me back to the ship?" I asked. It didn't really make any sense, but what the hell do I know about insane rock and roll space pirates. MC's smile stretched out, seeming to encompass his entire skull.

"There's a bounty for you on Pharosis. I intend to collect. Then maybe I'll kill you." He laughed as he made his way back up to the cockpit. The engines roared to life and we were on the move.

Awesome.

"That uh…that was a lot," reckoned one of the large men toward the end of the bar.

I had ramped up a bit at the end and though my drink was empty, I hadn't noticed. On top of that everyone else had simply gone quiet and was listening anxiously.

"It definitely wasn't my favorite visit to a strip club, but surprisingly, it wasn't my worst." I told them, leaning back and motioning to the bartender. A few new faces had joined us and at this point we were getting fairly chummy with each other.

"Still no girl, no Farrah," the gal behind the bar quipped.

"No, not yet. She's coming right up though." I confirmed. The bartender handed me the requested drink and set a tall dark shot next to it.

"On the house. This shit is great for business." He told me with a wink.

"So, are we getting to the venom, and the snakes, and all that? Besides, how exactly did you get away from ole Murder…eh-" The man next to me glanced at the blonde behind the bar. "MC anyway?"

"That's next, man. Let me drain the weasel and I'll be right back."

THE END OF BOOK ONE
TO BE CONTINUED IN
SATURN IS FOR SUCKERS BOOK TWO

Saturn is for Suckers

Made in the USA
Columbia, SC
09 March 2020